Viagra Sildenaf

The Medical Best Guide to Instant, Fast Acting, and Long Time (Long Lasting) Erection for Blue Men Sex for Her Screaming Mind Blowing Climax

KARIN ALMEIDA

Copyright @2023

Table of Contents

Chapter One

Introduction

Sildenafil citrate, the main component in Viagra, is used for more than just treating ED in males; it is also used to treat a variety of cardiac conditions. Viagra, also known by its generic name, sildenafil citrate, is a medicine (for example, pneumonic blood vessel hypertension). Revatio is just one of several brand names for the drug Viagra that are currently on the market.

The most common usage of Viagra today is for the treatment of erectile dysfunction. Viagra was initially developed to help reduce strain on the heart. Throughout the drug's history, Viagra has been found to have a significant and beneficial impact on how men rate the quality of their sexual experiences.

After taking Viagra as advised, its effects won't be felt for about 30 minutes. The time it takes for Viagra to take effect and how long it continues to work depend on a number of factors. The time it takes for Viagra to take action in your body and how long its effects endure are only two examples of such variables. These factors involve a wide range of items, including diet, general health, other drugs, underlying medical issues, and more. But of course, that's not all of them; there are many more.

Chapter Two

Viagra's Working Mechanism

Erectile dysfunction (also known as impotence) is a condition that affects males and is caused by a breakdown in communication between the penile nerves and the brain. This reduces blood flow to the corpora cavernosa, a pair of pliable structures that together form a chamber along the penis and are essential for achieving an erection. The medical term for men who struggle to maintain an erection is erectile dysfunction.

Viagra can improve blood flow to the areas of the penis involved for creating an erection. This means the patient has a better chance of achieving and keeping an erection. It accomplishes this by lowering intravenous pressure by relaxing vein walls. When taken, Viagra helps men get and keep an erection by boosting blood flow to the penis. Getting an erection will be much easier after reading this.

According to studies, the active ingredient in Viagra can begin working anywhere from 30 minutes to an hour after ingestion.

Getting an erection requires more than just popping a pill. For it to occur despite the obstacles, you must feel genuine enthusiasm for it. Maintaining calm and serenity while taking Viagra increases your chances of experiencing the drug's positive effects.

Patients with erectile dysfunction (those who have trouble obtaining or maintaining erections) who use Viagra simply increase their time spent in bed. For this reason, we may thank Viagra's method of action, which entails boosting circulation to the penile area. Erectile dysfunction refers to the inability to get or keep an erection in a satisfactory manner. An erection that has been harmed will not be restored. In such a case, you'll need to seek medical attention in a different way.

Two or three hours is the average time it takes for Viagra to start losing its effectiveness. This is right before its effectiveness begins to wane. Depending on the actions taken, the body's digestive processes, and the surrounding environmental factors, it may last for up to five hours. If it lasted more than five hours, that would be the case. An hour or more may pass before the active elements in Viagra begin helping men with erectile dysfunction keep an erection going. It is recommended that at least four hours pass between taking Viagra and engaging in sexual activity.

The frequency and duration of erections while Viagra is in your bloodstream depend on your body's ability to digest the drug.

The fact that Viagra does nothing to keep an erection from waning while it is in effect means that it will do nothing once you've reached your climax. This is because, once your erection hits its height, Viagra will do little to keep it there. Nonetheless, after reaching your climax, you may need a rest before you can get another erection. Because your blood supply may be decreasing, this may occur.

Though Viagra has numerous advantages, it cannot address the following problems:

± Early termination (coming too soon). Investigate whether or whether the treatment you're receiving is leading to premature release.

± Feeling physically and mentally spent after having sex. Consuming coffee is one of the best ways to minimize fatigue during sexual activity, while boosting general health is the most effective strategy. One of the best strategies to keep from getting sleepy when engaging in sexual activity is to drink coffee.

± Sex interests that are hardly detectable (low moxie). To combat this, you can either seek treatment or adopt different behaviors. The two choices are both viable.

Removal of all traces of Viagra from the body could take several hours. That's the norm, actually. However, the amount of time it takes for the chemical to leave your system entirely can be anywhere from five to six hours depending on how well you digest your food. Five to six hours may pass before the poison has left your system entirely. The severity of the necessary operations is also determined by other factors, such as how long it takes for the material to be eliminated from the body. The effects of a single 25-milligram (mg) dose may not be felt for two to three hours, while those of a 100-mg dose may take nearly three times as long to wear off. For a greater drug accumulation after a higher dose, this is necessary. This is due to the fact that increasing the dose causes a greater accumulation of medication in the body.

If you find that Viagra is not having the desired effect, increasing arousal via masturbation or foreplay may assist. You can maximize the benefits of Viagra by following these steps. If it doesn't begin functioning within the first half hour, don't take more than the daily dose suggested by your primary care physician. Because of the circumstances, this is the optimal solution. Retaining blood in the penis can lead to priapism, a painful erection that lasts longer than four hours and can damage penis tissue due to a lack of oxygen. In extreme cases, this could cause priapism. Consuming enough of fluids, foods high in magnesium, and foods high in potassium can help reduce priapism.

If something similar were to happen to you, you should get medical help as quickly as possible.

Chapter Three

Viagra Indications and Dosage

Different dosages of Viagra are required when the drug is used to treat pulmonary hypertension versus erectile dysfunction (that is, pulmonary arterial hypertension).

Viagra is available in 25 milligram, 50 milligram, and 100 milligram blue pills that resemble valuable stones. The name "Viagra" comes from the shape of the pill containing the drug. Viagra is an effective medicine for treating erectile dysfunction. One pill should be taken every 24 hours, anywhere from 30 minutes to an hour before sexual activity.

Viagra (Revatio) is a drug used to treat hypertension due to narrowing of the blood vessels. It is available in the form of round, white, film-coated capsules. Each 20mg pill should be taken every three hours, but never more frequently than once every three hours.

Joking about the dangers of taking too much Viagra is not funny. If you think you may have taken more than the suggested amount, you should get in touch with a doctor or a poison control center right once.

Listed below are some of the possible side effects of ingesting too much of a chemical:

- ± Vomiting
- ± Diarrhea
- ± Blindness
- ± A distorted and distorted vision and a damaged and scarred set of eyes.
- ± An injury to the nerves of the optic nerve (harm to the optic nerve)
- ± Extremely protracted and persistent priapism.
- ± It's been determined that papilledema exists (growing in the optic nerve)

- ± Perilous Heart Rate (that is expanded pulse)
- ± This condition is known as rhabdomyolysis (separate of muscles)

It's possible that you could die at any time, even though it's not something that typically occurs.

Before using Viagra or any other medicine that is similar to it to treat erectile dysfunction, you must have a full discussion with your primary care physician.

Viagra may interact negatively with a variety of other medications that are recommended for the treatment of heart conditions. Nitroglycerin and a range of other nitrates are among the medications in this class. The combination of these two likely results in a considerable drop in blood pressure.

Chapter Four

Factors with Impact on Viagra

Along with the dosage and frequency with which it is taken, additional variables affect Viagra's efficacy and duration of action in any given individual.

Diet

Viagra absorption is slowed or impeded by eating a very fatty or rich meal shortly before taking it. A healthy erection will be more challenging to achieve and keep going. But if you utilize it during your supper, you can reap the benefit of elongating its shelf life.

There will be a quicker response to the drug if it is taken on an empty stomach first thing in the morning.

Booze

Alcohol decreases the flow of blood to the penis, which makes it more difficult to achieve and keep an erection once it has formed. While using Viagra, consuming large quantities of alcohol can increase your risk of experiencing negative side effects, including the inability to get or keep an erection.

Age

The digestive system of an aged person often loosens up and becomes less stiff as they age. For men over the age of 65, there is a possibility that certain symptoms will last for a further two to three years.

Dosage

The length of time Viagra remains in your system is inversely proportional to the dose you initially took. Higher doses typically produce better effects that last longer. Talk to your family doctor about the right dosage, as it may not be safe to take more than the recommended amount. The appropriate dosage for you will be determined by your primary care physician.

Medications

Antibacterial drugs such as clarithromycin (Biaxin), erythromycin (Ery-Tab), and ciprofloxacin (Cipro) may decrease or prolong Viagra's effects. Get in touch with your primary care physician very away to find out whether there is a risk of drug interactions between the medications you are currently taking.

Mental Wellness

The level of discomfort, anxiety, stress, or misery in your life might alter your body's response to sexual desire. Any of these situations may diminish or shorten

Viagra's effectiveness. You should tell your doctor about any of these issues before using Viagra.

Wellbeing

Your body is undergoing changes that will determine the efficacy of Viagra and how long it will last for you. Conditions such as diabetes, issues with the sensory system like multiple sclerosis, and cardiac problems like atherosclerosis can all lessen Viagra's effectiveness and shorten its duration (fat buildup in the veins). Other neurological conditions, such as multiple sclerosis (MS), can also have this effect. This is a potential effect of other disorders that target the neurological system, such as lupus and lupus nephritis. An individual with certain hepatic or renal issues may experience Viagra's effects for far longer than they would in a healthy individual. Since it's necessary to separate the components of Viagra, this is the result.

Chapter Five

Viagra's Safety

If you use Viagra as prescribed and don't drink alcohol while taking it, you shouldn't have any major adverse effects. Still, there are concerns that eating it could cause a variety of negative health outcomes.

Preliminary clinical research has found that the majority of Viagra users have experienced the following side effects:

± A condition that causes visual impairment
± Indigestion
± Occlusion of the nose

± Light phobia (affectability to light)

± Headaches

Alternatively, the following are examples of what could be included in a response:

± Being hit with bad news out of the blue

± Rhythm disorders that originate in the lower heart chambers (the ventricles).

± An attack straight in the middle of the chest

± Excess fluid in the eye increases the pressure inside the eye.

± That Priapism (difficult dependable erection). Rarely

does something like this occur.

Some of our customers have told us that they have experienced cyanopsia on rare occasions. One symptom of cyanopsia is perceiving all colors as having a bluish cast. Having this form of colorblindness is indicated by cyanopsia.

Nonarthritic foremost ischemic optic neuropathy has also been associated to Viagra usage, but rarely. The loss of vision in one's affected eye(s) gets progressively worse with this type of optic neuropathy (that is harm to the optic nerve).

Consistent usage of Viagra has been related to sudden vision loss due to a reduction in blood flow to the optic nerve. Anecdotal evidence supports these assertions. Although extremely uncommon, the problem is more common in those with certain risk factors, such as diabetes, high cholesterol, a history of eye difficulties, cardiovascular disease, or high blood pressure.

People who are on protease inhibitors to control their HIV should talk to their primary care physician as soon as possible about the possibility of using Viagra. Inhibitors of proteases boost the frequency and intensity of responses. In this case, the maximum safe dosage of Viagra is 25 milligrams, which should not be used at once or within 48 hours of each other.

Taking Viagra at least four hours before or after taking alpha-blockers will also help prevent a dangerously low pulse rate in people who take both medications. As a result, fewer people will have a heart attack. A cardiac arrest can be avoided if this is done in time.

Chapter Six

Viagra Should Be Avoided By

It is not possible to make Viagra available to everyone as a treatment option because of how expensive it is. The target demographic for this product is made up of male adults (18+) who identify as such. Under no circumstances can women or children consume. Perhaps neither of the two groups will take this step.

Viagra users are strongly discouraged from attending social events without first consulting their family doctor.

- ± Chronic liver disease or heart disease patients
- ± Long-staying hospital patients who have had a prior stroke or heart failure
- ± Those who have been diagnosed with kidney disease
- ± Patients with inherited forms of retinal degeneration (that is individuals with uncommon acquired eye infection)
- ± Individuals suffering from hypotension, often known as low blood pressure (low circulatory strain)
- ± Individuals who use nitrates for chest pain relief and later

drink nitric oxide boosters, nitrates, or natural nitrites. people who take preventative measures to alleviate chest pain by taking nitrates.

± If a patient has ever had a bad reaction to Viagra or any of the other meds in this treatment, they can't have it again. people who did not improve while taking each medication separately or while taking one of the alternatives, such Viagra.

± Men should exercise some degree of self-preservation and refrain from sexual engagement if they have been warned of the elevated risk of cardiovascular disease.

WORTHY OF NOTE

Viagra Should Be Avoided By

It is not possible to make Viagra available to everyone as a treatment option because of how expensive it is. The target demographic for this product is made up of male adults (18+) who identify as such. Under no circumstances can women or children consume. Perhaps neither of the two groups will take this step.

Viagra users are strongly discouraged from attending social events without first consulting their family doctor.

- ± Chronic liver disease or heart disease patients
- ± Long-staying hospital patients who have had a prior stroke or heart failure
- ± Those who have been diagnosed with kidney disease
- ± Patients with inherited forms of retinal degeneration (that is individuals with uncommon acquired eye infection)

± Individuals suffering from hypotension, often known as low blood pressure (low circulatory strain)

± Individuals who use nitrates for chest pain relief and later drink nitric oxide boosters, nitrates, or natural nitrites. people who take preventative measures to alleviate chest pain by taking nitrates.

± If a patient has ever had a bad reaction to Viagra or any of the other meds in this treatment, they can't have it again. people who did not improve while taking each medication separately or while taking one of the alternatives, such Viagra.

± Men should exercise some degree of self-preservation and refrain from sexual engagement if they have been warned of the elevated risk of cardiovascular disease.

Viagra's Safety

If you use Viagra as prescribed and don't drink alcohol while taking it, you shouldn't have any major adverse effects. Still, there are concerns that eating it could cause a variety of negative health outcomes.

Preliminary clinical research has found that the majority of Viagra users have experienced the following side effects:

- ± A condition that causes visual impairment
- ± Indigestion
- ± Occlusion of the nose
- ± Light phobia (affectability to light)
- ± Headaches

Alternatively, the following are examples of what could be included in a response:

- ± Being hit with bad news out of the blue

- ± Rhythm disorders that originate in the lower heart chambers (the ventricles).
- ± An attack straight in the middle of the chest
- ± Excess fluid in the eye increases the pressure inside the eye.
- ± That Priapism (difficult dependable erection). Rarely does something like this occur.

Some of our customers have told us that they have experienced cyanopsia on rare occasions. One symptom of cyanopsia is perceiving all colors as having a bluish cast. Having this form of colorblindness is indicated by cyanopsia.

Nonarthritic foremost ischemic optic neuropathy has also been associated to Viagra usage, but rarely. The loss of vision in one's affected eye(s) gets progressively worse with this type of optic neuropathy (that is harm to the optic nerve).

Consistent usage of Viagra has been related to sudden vision loss due to a reduction in blood flow to the optic nerve. Anecdotal evidence supports these assertions. Although extremely uncommon, the problem is more common in those with certain risk factors, such as diabetes, high cholesterol, a history of eye difficulties, cardiovascular disease, or high blood pressure.

People who are on protease inhibitors to control their HIV should talk to their primary care physician as soon as possible about the possibility of using Viagra. Inhibitors of proteases boost the frequency and intensity of responses. In this case, the maximum safe dosage of Viagra is 25 milligrams, which should not be used at once or within 48 hours of each other.

Taking Viagra at least four hours before or after taking alpha-blockers will also help prevent a dangerously low pulse rate in people who take both medications. As a result, fewer people will have a heart attack. A cardiac arrest can be avoided if this is done in time.

Viagra Indications and Dosage

Different dosages of Viagra are required when the drug is used to treat pulmonary hypertension versus erectile dysfunction (that is, pulmonary arterial hypertension).

Viagra is available in 25 milligram, 50 milligram, and 100 milligram blue pills that resemble valuable stones. The name "Viagra" comes from the shape of the pill containing the drug. Viagra is an effective medicine for treating erectile dysfunction. One pill should be taken every 24 hours, anywhere from 30 minutes to an hour before sexual activity.

Viagra (Revatio) is a drug used to treat hypertension due to narrowing of the blood vessels. It is available in the form of round, white, film-coated capsules. Each 20mg pill should be taken every three hours, but never more frequently than once every three hours.

Joking about the dangers of taking too much Viagra is not funny. If you think you may have taken more than the suggested amount, you should get in touch with a doctor or a poison control center right once.

Listed below are some of the possible side effects of ingesting too much of a chemical:

- ± Vomiting
- ± Diarrhea
- ± Blindness
- ± A distorted and distorted vision and a damaged and scarred set of eyes.
- ± An injury to the nerves of the optic nerve (harm to the optic nerve)

- ± Extremely protracted and persistent priapism.
- ± It's been determined that papilledema exists (growing in the optic nerve)
- ± Perilous Heart Rate (that is expanded pulse)
- ± This condition is known as rhabdomyolysis (separate of muscles)

It's possible that you could die at any time, even though it's not something that typically occurs.

Before using Viagra or any other medicine that is similar to it to treat erectile dysfunction, you must have a full discussion with your primary care physician.

Viagra may interact negatively with a variety of other medications that are recommended for the treatment of heart conditions. Nitroglycerin and a range of other nitrates are among the medications in this class. The combination of these two likely results in a considerable drop in blood pressure.

Printed in Great Britain
by Amazon